CreativeKiDs
publishing

Jack and the Beanstalk

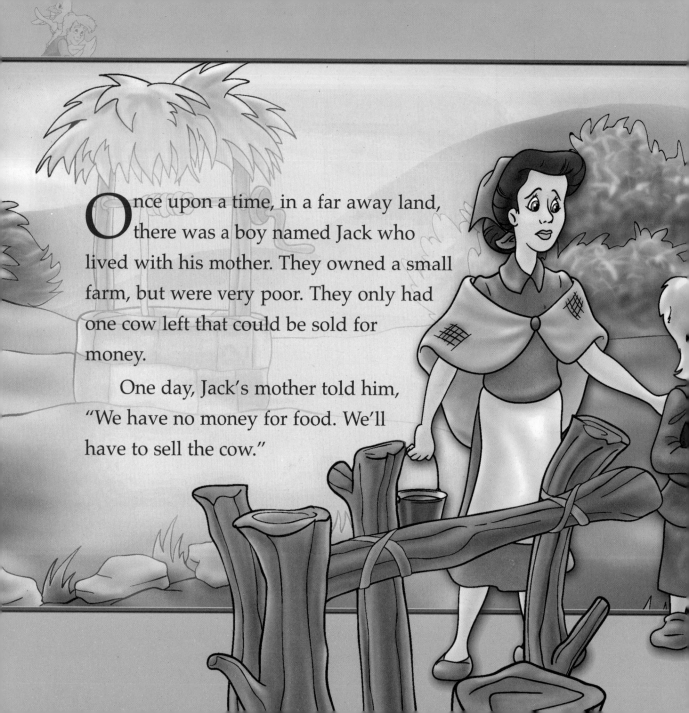

Once upon a time, in a far away land, there was a boy named Jack who lived with his mother. They owned a small farm, but were very poor. They only had one cow left that could be sold for money.

One day, Jack's mother told him, "We have no money for food. We'll have to sell the cow."

Jack took the cow to the market. On the way, he met a man. "If you give me your cow," said the man, "I'll give you some magic beans that are better than money."

Jack thought the magic beans sounded wonderful, so he gave the man the cow, and ran home as fast as he could.

Jack's mother was surprised to see her son return so quickly from the market. "How much did you get for the cow?" she asked.

"I got something much better than money," explained Jack proudly, showing her the magic beans.

"Beans! These beans are no good to us!" cried his mother angrily, and she threw them out the window.

When Jack awoke the next morning, he looked out the window and saw that a huge beanstalk had grown from the magic beans overnight.

"I must find out what's at the top," he cried and rushed outside. Up and up he climbed through the clouds. At last, he reached the top and found a long road that led to a huge castle.

Jack knocked on the enormous door of the castle but no one answered. Then, he pushed on the very heavy door and it slowly creaked open. Jack was sure a giant lived there. Everything in the castle was giant-sized and towered above him as he looked around.

Suddenly, Jack heard loud footsteps coming his way. *BOOM, BOOM, BOOM!*

Jack quickly hid in a cupboard. He carefully peeked out and saw a fierce giant!

The giant sniffed the air. "Fee, fie, foe, fum, I smell the blood of an Englishman! Be he alive or be he dead, I'll grind his bones to make my bread!" he roared. The giant looked around, but could not find Jack.

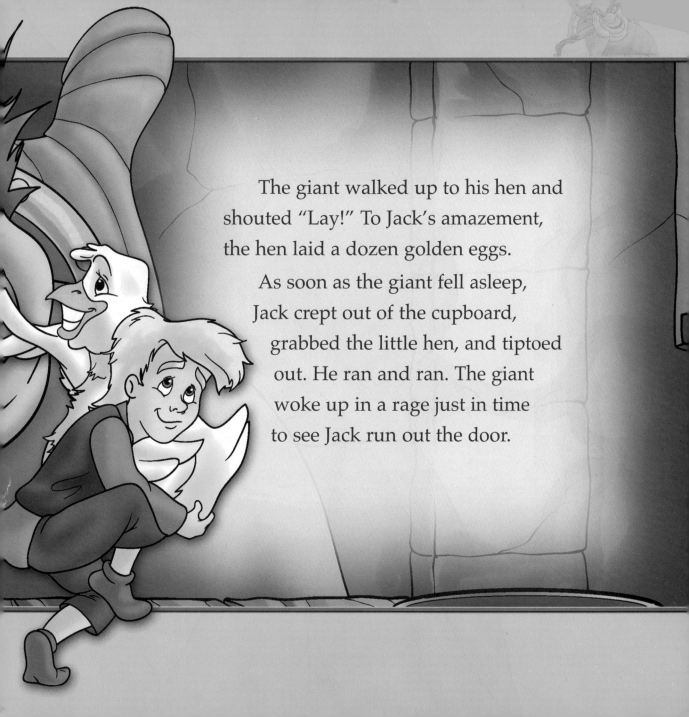

The giant walked up to his hen and shouted "Lay!" To Jack's amazement, the hen laid a dozen golden eggs.

As soon as the giant fell asleep, Jack crept out of the cupboard, grabbed the little hen, and tiptoed out. He ran and ran. The giant woke up in a rage just in time to see Jack run out the door.

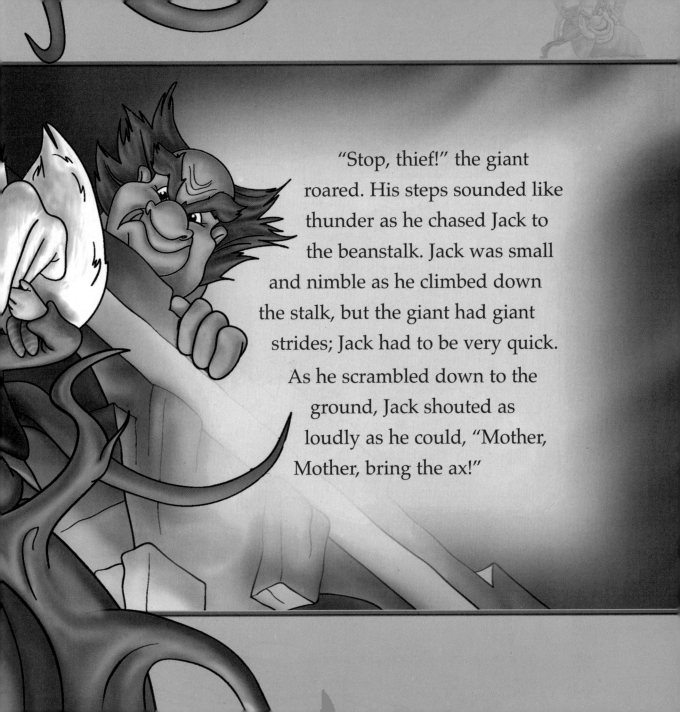

"Stop, thief!" the giant roared. His steps sounded like thunder as he chased Jack to the beanstalk. Jack was small and nimble as he climbed down the stalk, but the giant had giant strides; Jack had to be very quick. As he scrambled down to the ground, Jack shouted as loudly as he could, "Mother, Mother, bring the ax!"

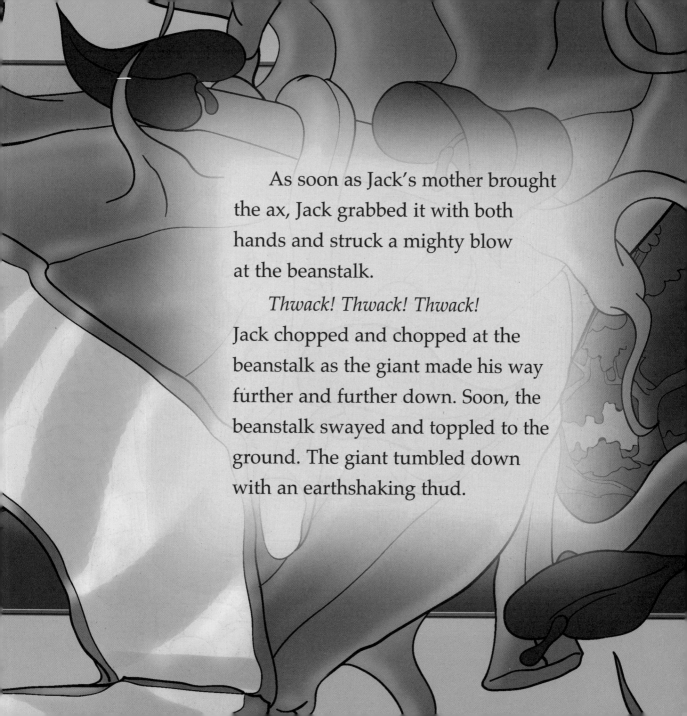

As soon as Jack's mother brought the ax, Jack grabbed it with both hands and struck a mighty blow at the beanstalk.

Thwack! Thwack! Thwack! Jack chopped and chopped at the beanstalk as the giant made his way further and further down. Soon, the beanstalk swayed and toppled to the ground. The giant tumbled down with an earthshaking thud.